Rosa's

Room

To my friend with the kite

—B. B.

In loving memory of my mom, Dorothy

—B. S.

Rosa's Room

Written by

Barbara Bottner

Illustrated by

Beth Spiegel

PEACHTREE
ATLANTA

Rosa had a new room in a new house.

It seemed empty.

On Monday, Rosa took out her crayons
and put them in a drawer in her desk.

She hung her clothes in her closet.
She unpacked her doll, Maria, and laid her on the bed.

On Tuesday, Rosa found her treasure box,
the one her father had made. She placed it on her desk.

Then she unwrapped her teapot,
while her cat Concertina looked on.

Rosa looked around.
Her room was still too empty.

That night, as Rosa went to sleep,
she wondered what else she could do to decorate her room.

On Wednesday, Rosa's new teacher gave her a poster for Book Day. It fit perfectly on Rosa's wall, just between the door and the bookcase.

On Thursday, Rosa's mother took her to the library.
Rosa borrowed five new books.
She placed them around her room.

On Friday, when Rosa was in the park,
she thought about her room some more.

That night, Rosa dreamed of
something beautiful
to cover her bed.

On Saturday, Rosa's mother bought some flowered material, and together they made a bedspread that fit just right.

“My room looks better,” Rosa whispered to Concertina.
But Concertina sat in the middle of the room.
“More,” the cat seemed to say.

On Sunday, when Rosa was drawing
a picture, she saw a girl outside.
That gave her an idea.

"My name is Lili," said the girl with the kite.
Rosa invited her to come see her room.

Lili loved kites, butterflies, and drawing. She loved Maria, Concertina, and every single thing that was in Rosa's room.

Especially Rosa.

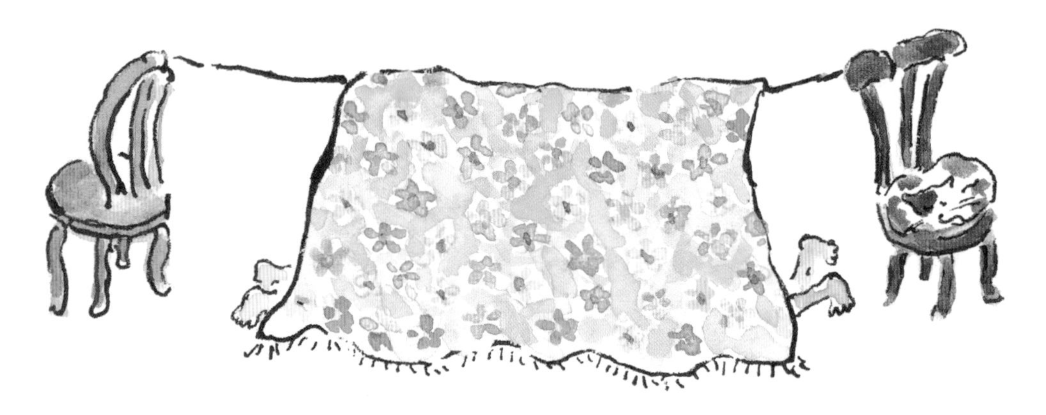

Published by
PEACHTREE PUBLISHERS
1700 Chattahoochee Avenue
Atlanta, Georgia 30318-2112
www.peachtree-online.com

First trade paperback edition published in 2013

10 9 8 7 6 5 4 3 2 1 (hardcover)
10 9 8 7 6 5 4 3 2 1 (trade paperback)

Printed in July 2013 by Imago in China

Art direction by Loraine M. Joyner
Composition by Melanie McMahon Ives
Title calligraphy by Liz Manera

Paintings created in watercolor, guache, and India ink on acid-free 100% rag paper
Text typeset in Baskerville Infant

Library of Congress Cataloging-in-Publication Data

Bottner, Barbara.
Rosa's room / written by Barbara Bottner; illustrated by Beth Spiegel.-- 1st ed.
p. cm.
Summary: Rosa searches for things that will fill her room in her new home, but it feels empty until she discovers exactly what is missing.

ISBN 978-1-56145-302-3 / 1-56145-302-1 (hardcover)
ISBN 978-1-56145-776-2 / 1-56145-776-0 (trade paperback)

[1. Bedrooms--Fiction. 2. Moving, Household--Fiction. 3. Friendship--Fiction.]
I. Spiegel, Beth, 1957- ill. II. Title.
PZ7.B6586 Ro 2004
[E]--dc22 2003016837